Happy Cat First Readers

# WHAT DINO SAW

VICTOR
KELLEHER

ILLUSTRATED BY
TOM JELLETT

HAPPY CAT BOOKS

Published by
Happy Cat Books
An imprint of Catnip Publishing Ltd
14 Greville Street
London EC1N 8SB

First published by Penguin Books, Australia, 2004

This edition first published 2008
1 3 5 7 9 10 8 6 4 2

A CIP catalogue record for this book is available from the
British Library

ISBN  978-1-905117-80-2

Printed in Poland

www.catnippublishing.co.uk

For Luke, Beth, and Jacob. *V.K.*

For Frank and his strange theories

on the T-Rex that the world isn't

ready for . . . just yet. *T.J.*

# Chapter One

Jenny found a big egg-
shaped thing down by the
river. It made a funny noise
when she picked
it up.

'Beep,' it said. (Which
means, 'Let me out of here.')

She tried showing it to

her dad, but he was busy making lunch.

'Don't bother me now, love,' he said.

She showed it to her mum, but she was busy at the computer.

'I'll look in a few minutes,' she said.

Jenny knew what a few minutes meant. So she took the egg-thing and put it in the airing cupboard.

'Bee-eep,' it said. (Which
means, 'This feels like a
nice warm place.')

When she went to check
on it later, it was starting to
hatch. It had cracked all

3

over. One of the cracks grew so wide that the egg split in two. Out popped a creature with a long tail and green eyes. It was a bit like a dragon and a lot like a baby dinosaur.

It looked up, searching for its mum. And what it saw was Jenny.

'Bleep,' it said. (In dinosaur-talk that means, 'You must be my mum.')

When Jenny walked off along the passage, it ran after her. It followed her up to her bedroom and back down to the garden. Then it followed her three times around the house.

It followed her everywhere!

'Boop,' it kept saying. (Which means, 'Wait for me, Mum.')

Jenny decided to call him Dino.

She took him back to
Dad, who was busy cooking
dinner now.

'This isn't a good time
for me, love,' he said.

She and Dino looked in

on Mum, who was
answering her email.

'I'll be with you in half
an hour,' she said.

Jenny knew what half an
hour meant too. So she and

Dino went out into the garden.

For a baby, Dino seemed pretty hungry. First, he ate most of the back lawn.

Next, the washing on the line and a bag of clothes pegs. (He really liked the clothes pegs.) After that, he gobbled up the rose bushes, the door of the shed and a small tree.

'Bur-urp,' he said.

That wasn't dinosaur-talk. It's what everyone says after a meal.

# Chapter Two

Mum and Dad didn't talk much at dinner that night. Dad was busy studying a new cookbook. Mum was reading about some software for her computer.

'What do you think of Dino?' Jenny asked them.

'Mmm . . . er . . . hang on
a minute,' Mum said.

'Mmm . . . er . . . what
was that, love?' Dad said.

Dino looked at Jenny's

mum and dad. 'Blee-oop,'
he said. (Which means,
'Who are those weirdos
with my mum?')

While the family was
finishing dinner, Dino
decided to have a small
snack. He went into the
lounge and ate Mum's
favourite rug. Then he ate
the curtains, the pot plants,
all the photo albums (they
weren't as tasty as the

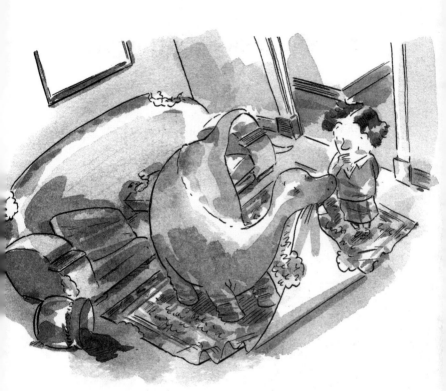

clothes pegs), the cushions
on the sofa, the lounge door
and one of the armchairs.
He nearly ate the cat too,

but she escaped through
the window.

'Er . . . mm . . . what's all

that noise?' Dad muttered, his nose still in his book.

'Mmm . . . er . . . haven't a clue,' Mum said. 'Must be the neighbours.'

'Mmm . . . er . . . you're probably right,' Dad agreed.

Round about then, Jenny noticed how much Dino had grown. He was a *lot* bigger.

'It's the garden for you tonight,' she said, and locked him outside.

'Blee-ee-eep!' he wailed.
(Which means, 'My mum
doesn't love me!')

He was so upset that he
had another meal. He ate
the front lawn, the fruit
trees, the rest of the shed,
the clothes line, both side
fences, the wooden floor of
the veranda, the garage
doors and everything in the
veggie garden. He washed
it all down with the water

from the neighbours'
swimming pool.

Then he closed his eyes
with a sigh.

'Bap-eeee-bap-eeee-bap-
eee,' he said.

Which doesn't mean
anything. It's just the noise
dinosaurs make when they
snore.

# Chapter Three

Dino grew some more
during the night.
By morning he was as
big as a car.

He looked extra happy
when Jenny came out of
the house.

'Bloopee!' he cried.

(Which means, 'Mum loves

me again!')

He followed her all the

way to school.

They took quite a long

time to get there. Mainly
because Dino had to keep
stopping for snacks. Hedges
were what he liked best. He
ate a lot of those. Rubbish
bins too. It was rubbish
collection day, so there were
plenty to choose from.

They arrived at school
late. The teacher was really
angry.

'What kind of time do you
call this?' she said.

Jenny tried explaining about Dino, but the teacher wouldn't listen.

'Don't give me any of your silly excuses,' she said.

Jenny pointed towards the window. Dino was right outside, his big wet nose pressed against the glass. But the teacher had already turned her back. She was busy writing on the blackboard.

'I don't have time for gazing out of windows,' she said. 'I have a class to teach.'

The other kids had plenty

of time to gaze out of
windows. It was what they
did most of the day.

'Hey!' they'd shout. 'Dino's
just eaten the goal posts.'

Or: 'He's starting on the trees now.'

Or: 'Well, that's the last of the sports sheds.'

Or: 'I think he's drunk the river dry.'

The teacher wasn't pleased with them. She reckoned they were the worst class she'd ever had.

'You haven't listened to a word I've said all day,' she scolded them.

'Yes, Miss,' they agreed, and went on watching Dino, who had begun chomping his way through the bike sheds.

# Chapter Four

Dino was waiting outside
when the bell rang. The
minute he saw Jenny, he
came rushing across the car
park.

'Blip-blip,' he said.
(Which means, 'I've missed
you heaps.')

'Oh, dear!' Jenny said, because he'd flattened the teachers' cars.

He'd gone on growing during the day. He was bigger than a bus now.

None of the teachers noticed him because they were too busy looking at what was left of their cars.

'Someone will have to pay for this,' the principal said.

Jenny didn't like the sound of that. She took Dino off to the park.

Lots of little kids were there with their parents. The parents were sitting on benches, talking together.

'Hey, Mum! Hey, Dad! Check out the dinosaur!' the kids shouted.

'Mmm . . . er . . . yes, dear,' the parents said, and went on chatting.

The kids thought Dino was great. For a while anyway. Until he ate their playground equipment. (He enjoyed the slide most of all.) He followed that up with a climbing frame, ten

scooters, five skateboards
and a brand new bike.

**'Waaagh!'** said the kids.
'The dinosaur swallowed
our stuff!'

'Don't interrupt,' the
parents said. 'Can't you see
we're talking?'

That was when the park
keeper came along. He
looked puzzled.

'I could have sworn there
were trees and bushes

around here,' he said. 'I seem
to remember a lake too.'

Jenny thought it was a
good time to take Dino
home.

He squashed a few more

cars on the way. He also
flattened three bus
shelters, two post boxes and
a row of lamp posts.

He only just squeezed
along the street where

Jenny lived. And he hardly
fitted into her front garden.
He had to rest his head on
a telegraph pole and curl
his tail around the
neighbours' garage.

'Bee-leep,' he said. (Which means, 'Why is everything getting smaller?')

Jenny wondered what he'd find to eat during the night. The garden was already looking bare.

But she needn't have worried. There was still plenty of house left.

# Chapter Five

'Brrr!' said Dad when he woke next morning. 'It's a chilly one.'

'Yes, and damp,' Mum said.

She was right. Rain was sprinkling on their heads.

'What happened to the roof?' Dad said.

He and Mum went into the bathroom.

'Where did the shower go?' Mum asked.

'And the bath and basin?' Dad added.

They couldn't find the wardrobe either. Or any of their clothes. They took the bedsheets and wrapped themselves in those.

'I think we're having one of those bad days you hear about,' Mum said.

'You're not wrong,' Dad said.

When they tried to go downstairs, the stairs had disappeared. They had to tie their sheets together and climb down.

'Are you sure we're awake?' Dad asked.

'I hope not,' Mum answered.

It was just as rainy
downstairs. They looked
for the lounge, but there
wasn't one. The dining
room had disappeared with
it. And what had happened
to the front door and
veranda?

The thing that really
bothered Dad was the
kitchen. Mostly it was
empty space. The stove and
microwave had gone. The

fridge and cupboards had
gone. The sink was still
there, but with teeth marks
around the edge.

'My cookbooks!' Dad

sobbed. 'Someone's taken them!'

Mum opened the door to where her office had been. 'My computer!' she

wailed. 'Someone's stolen it!'

They dried their eyes and gazed sadly through the rain. They could see something in the garden. It looked like one of those blow-up animals you can buy.

But **HUGE!**

'Who left a blimp out there?' they asked together.

'It's not a blimp,' someone answered. 'This is Dino.'

They blinked and looked
harder. Jenny was standing

under the blow-up thing.
Its front paw was keeping
her dry.

'Dino?' Mum said. 'What's
a Dino?'

'I've told you,' Jenny
said. 'Dino's my pet
dinosaur.'

'Well, get rid of it,' Dad
said. 'We have enough to
worry about without plastic
animals. And it's ruining
the garden.'

'Yes,' Mum said. 'Let the air out of it, and put it in the rubbish.'

'Bur-urp,' said Dino.

'Not that kind of air,' said Dad.

# Chapter Six

Jenny took Dino down to
the river. It was a very big
river. Dino really liked it.

'Beepo,' he said. (Which
means, 'Look at all that
yummy weed.')

He splashed straight in
and swam towards the sea.
'Boople-pip,' he called
back. (Which means, 'Sorry,
Mum, time to leave home.')

Jenny was sad to see him go. On the other hand, she always knew where he was. There was stuff about him in the newspaper nearly every week:

**Monster eats hotel on north coast. Hundreds flee.**

the headlines declared.

Or:

**Monster eats police station on south coast. Hundreds flee again.**

'Look, Mum. Look, Dad,'
Jenny would say. 'It's Dino.'
But they were busy with

their new house now, and
their new computer, and
their new kitchen.

'Mmm . . . er . . . yes,

dear,' Mum would say as
she surfed the net.

'Mmm . . . er . . . yes, love,'
Dad would say, as he

checked the cake he was baking.

Jenny didn't mind about any of that. She did miss Dino, though. She spent most of her time down at the river where she'd found him.

She was looking for egg-shaped stones. The sort that say 'Beep' when you pick them up.

## Chapter Seven

Then one day Jenny was late home for dinner.

'Where's that girl got to?' Dad wondered.

Mum looked out of the window. There was Jenny, sitting happily on the back lawn. She wasn't alone.

'Oh, dear,' Mum said.
'She's brought home
another one!'

'Not another blow-up
dinosaur,' Dad complained.

He also gazed out of the
window. *This* dinosaur was
much fiercer looking than
the first. It had big hungry
jaws, lots of pointy teeth
and the sharpest claws Dad
had ever seen.

'What do you think of

Rex?' Jenny called out.

'**Bleep!**' roared Rex when Jenny patted him. (In T-Rex talk that means, 'You're my mum, and don't anyone contradict me.')

'It's amazing what they can do with plastic toys these days,' Dad said nervously.

'Amazing or not,' Mum said, 'it can't stay like that. Tell her to let

the air out, or it will scare
the neighbours.'

'Right you are,' Dad said,
and reached for the door.

Except there wasn't one.

The back door had vanished. So had the back veranda, the clothes line, the garden shed, the rose bushes, the new hedge, half

the garage and the dog
kennel, dog included.

There was no sign of the
neighbours either.

Dad scratched his head

and took another look at
Rex. He took a *long*, *hard*
look this time. He couldn't
help noticing how *real* Rex

seemed. How *alive*! And how easily he crunched up the rest of the garage!

'Tell you what,' Dad said in a worried voice, and hid behind the sofa. 'I think I know where the back door went. And the neighbours too.'

Mum had also seen the garage disappear. She chose to hide under the table.

'Hey, Mum. Hey, Dad,'

Jenny called. 'Come and meet Rex.'

'No way!' Mum and Dad said together.

## From Victor Kelleher

I was reading the other day about animals that hatch from eggs. Often, they think the first thing they see is their mum. Try it with newly hatched baby geese. They'll follow you everywhere – the way Dino follows Jenny. I reckon the first thing most people see is a picture of dinosaurs. That would explain why we love them so.

## From Tom Jellett

I'm not sure where I would keep a dinosaur if I had one as a pet. I haven't got a very large backyard, so I would have to take it down to the park for walkies. This might unsettle the other dogs and their owners in the park, and the café owners would have to make a much larger 'pupaccino' than usual. If my dinosaur was as hungry as Jenny's, then it wouldn't stop at a focaccia, it would probably eat the café as well . . .

*Look out for these other
Happy Cat First Readers.*

# The Princess and the Unicorn

Wendy Blaxland

No one believes in unicorns any more. Except Princess Lily, that is.
So when the king falls ill and the only thing that can cure him is
the magic of a unicorn, it's up to her to find one.
But can Lily find a magical unicorn in time?

Becky was cross with her little brother. 'If you don't leave me alone,' she said to him, 'I'll put a spell on you!' But she didn't mean to make him disappear!

Crystal longs to be a mermaid.
Her mother makes her a flashing silver tail. But it isn't like
being a proper mermaid. Then one night Crystal wears her
tail to bed...

Jock can make a special sound like a duck!
If you can learn to make it too you can help Jock rescue the
little duck from the duck hunter. Quick, before it's too late!

David's had a party invitation!
It's a dressing-up party and he's going to go as a fox. But
when he arrives he can see he's made a mistake in choosing
his costume. Can he still fit in with the party theme and
have fun?

Nicholas Nosh is the littlest pirate in the world. He's not allowed to go to sea. 'You're too small,' said his dad. But when the fierce pirate Captain Red Beard kidnaps his family, Nicholas sets sail to rescue them!

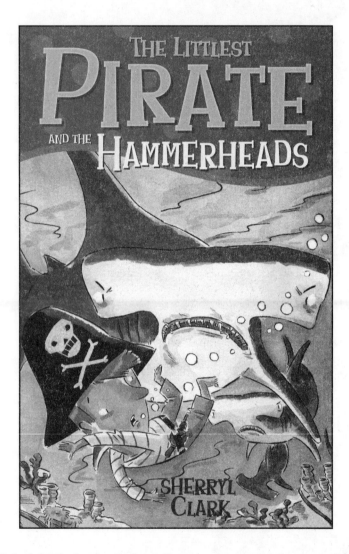

Nicholas Nosh, the littlest pirate in the world, has to rescue his family's treasure which has been stolen by Captain Hammerhead. But how can he outwit the sharks that are guarding Captain Hammerhead's ship?

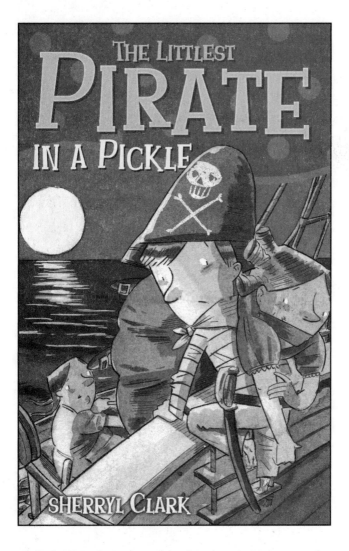

THE LITTLEST
PIRATE
IN A PICKLE

SHERRYL CLARK

Nicholas Nosh is teased by his cousin Primrose for
being so small. But when Captain Manners of the
Jolly Dodger kidnaps her, Nicholas shows just how
brave a little pirate he can be!

When Anna
Slept Over

Jane Godwin

Josie is Anna's best friend. Anna has played at Josie's house,
she's even stayed for dinner, but she has never slept over.
Until now…

Tom was given a gorilla suit for his birthday. He loved it and wore it everywhere. When mum and dad took him to the zoo he wouldn't wear his ordinary clothes. But isn't it asking for trouble to go to the zoo dressed as a gorilla?

First day at new school for Kerry.
It's easy to get lost in a big new school when you don't
know anyone. But a helpful dog shows Kerry the way to the
playground - and to lots of new friends!